Doodling Daniel

By Joyce Dunbar

Illustrated by James Dunbar

Daniel liked to doodle. He did ...

... hairy doodles   ... spiky doodles

... bouncy doodles   ... loopy doodles.

Sometimes he did lots of doodles in a row and made them look ...

... happy ... or sad.

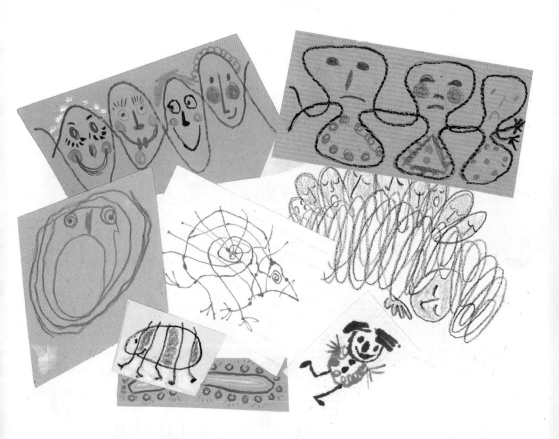

He did oodles and oodles of doodles.

Then one day he doodled a door ...

... and went through it.

He stood in a vast empty space.

So he doodled himself a tree ...

... and climbed up it.

7

He couldn't get down so he
doodled himself a flying machine.

He flew through the clouds to a

doodled desert island. 9

He suddenly felt very lonely so he doodled a Doodledog and some friendly loopy creatures.

He wanted to get off the island so he doodled some water around it and a boat.

But all the strange friendly loopies wanted to come too and they scrambled aboard and tipped up the boat ...

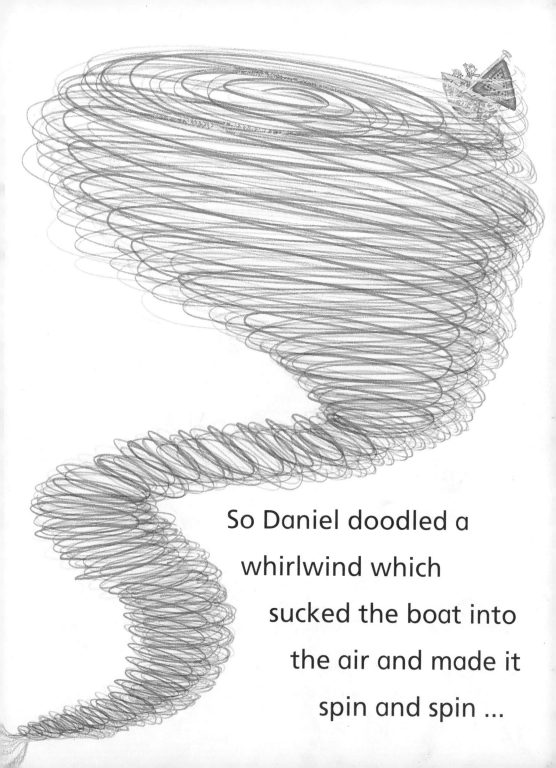

So Daniel doodled a
whirlwind which
sucked the boat into
the air and made it
spin and spin ...

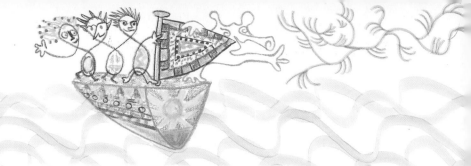

... and fall and fall and sink and sink ...

... until Daniel stood in the doodled
depths of the doodled ocean and
there met ...

... the Doodler of the deep.

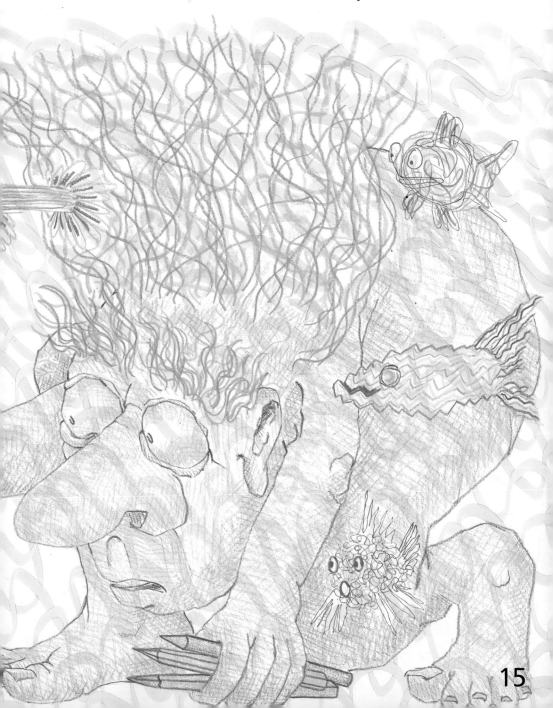

Daniel felt afraid of the Doodler so
he doodled a dinosaur so big and

thirsty that it drank all the water in the sea ...

... and took Daniel to a land where everyone and everything was doodled.

18

Daniel doodled presents for everyone and a great big tea.

"Take me home now," he said to the dinosaur.

20

And the dinosaur carried him back to
the vast empty space ...
with a door ...

Daniel went through it ...

... and found that Doodledog had
followed him home.

This book is part of

THE LONGMAN BOOK PROJECT

General Editor Sue Palmer
Fiction Editor Wendy Body
Non-fiction Editor Bobbie Neate

PEARSON EDUCATION LIMITED
Edinburgh Gate, Harlow, Essex, CM20 2JE, England and
Associated Companies throughout the World.

First published 1994
Fourth impression 1999
ISBN 0 582 12090 X

Also available in larger format
ISBN 0582 12083 7

Set in LeFrut 28/44pt (Linotronic)
Printed in Singapore (HBM)

The publisher's policy is to use paper manufactured from sustainable forests.

Some other books by
Joyce and James Dunbar

Why is the sky up?
published by Dent

I want a blue banana
published by Dent

Joyce Dunbar has also written:

A Bun for Barney
published by Corgi

Spring Rabbit
published by Anderson

Five mice and the moon
published by Orchard

I wish I liked rice pudding
published by Simon and Schuster

Mouse and Mole
published by Doubleday